CREEPY MONSTERS, SLEEPY MONSTERS

 *a lullaby*

JANE YOLEN

illustrated by KELLY MURPHY

CANDLEWICK PRESS

First edition 2011

Library of Congress Cataloging-in-Publication Data is available.

Library of Congress Catalog Card Number pending

ISBN 978-0-7636-4201-3

11 12 13 14 15 16 CCP 10 9 8 7 6 5 4 3 2 1

Printed in Shenzhen, Guangdong, China

This book was typeset in Wilke Bold.
The illustrations were done in oil, acrylic, and gel medium on paper.

Candlewick Press
99 Dover Street
Somerville, Massachusetts 02144

visit us at www.candlewick.com

For Susannah Richards,
who is neither creepy nor a monster
J.Y.

For Natalie, Brendan, Meredith, and Scott,
the Fairbanks monsters
K. M.

Monsters creep,
Monsters crawl,

Over the meadow

And up the wall.

Monsters run,

Monsters stumble,

Monsters hip-hop,
Monsters tumble,

Monsters slither,
Monsters wave,

All in a hurry
To get to their cave . . .

Where monsters grab
A bite to eat,

Then into the tub
To wash their feet,

Then monster prayers,

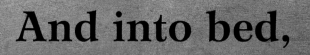

And into bed,

But they toss and turn
And bounce instead.

GROWL

Gurgle

SNARL

SNARF

I'm not sleepy.